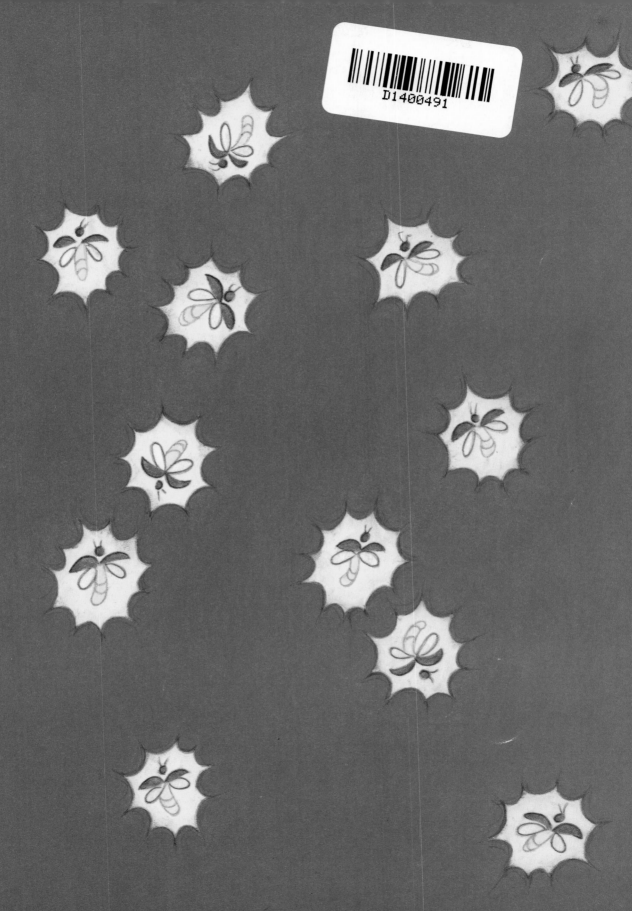

Night Fell at Harry's Farm

By Carey Hedlund

GREENWILLOW BOOKS, NEW YORK

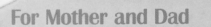

For Mother and Dad

Pastels were used for the full-color art.
The text type is Geometric 231.

Printed in Hong Kong by South China Printing Company (1988) Ltd.
First Edition   10 9 8 7 6 5 4 3 2 1

Library of Congress Cataloging-in-Publication Data

Hedlund, Carey.
Night fell at Harry's farm / by Carey Hedlund.
        p.   cm.
Summary: A visit to Harry's farm features dinner outside,
dancing fireflies, and scary stories by the fire.
ISBN 0-688-14932-4   [1. Country life—Fiction.]
I. Title.   PZ7.H3563Ni   1997
[E]—dc20   96-5414   CIP   AC

We drove from the city on curving roads.

We got lost.

ROUTE
22

DETOUR

NO
RIGHT
TURN

We had to stop because of a fire.
Once the flames were put out,
we asked for directions.

We should have turned left
at the bridge by the willow.

We finally found the road that we wanted.

First the road went through someone else's farm.

Then, just as it got dark, we got to Harry's.

The only light in the house

was the TV that no one was watching.

We found Harry out back
cooking our dinner.

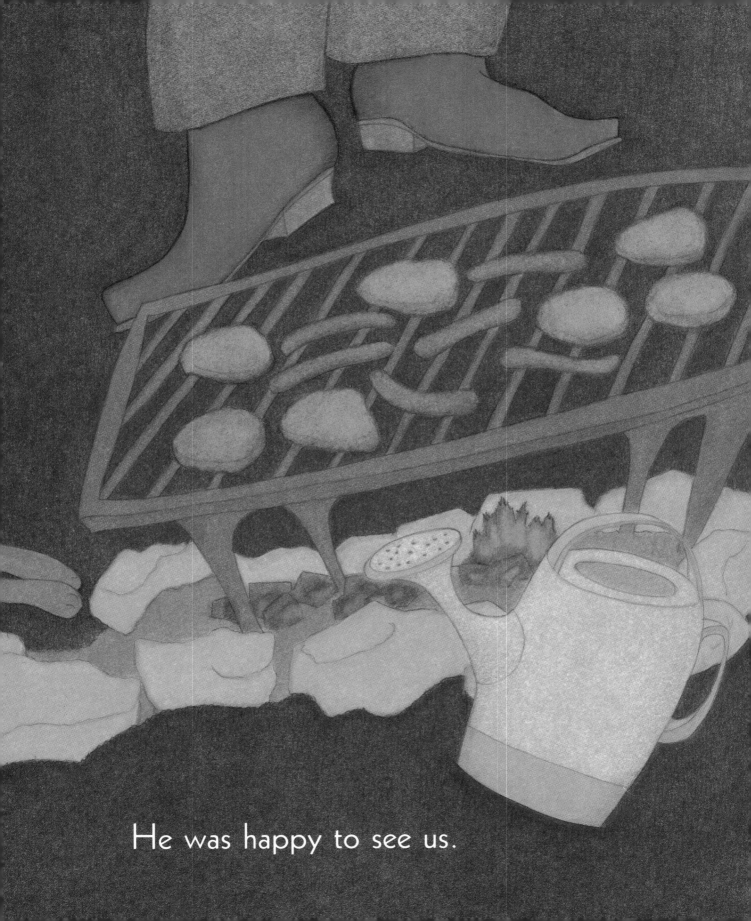

He was happy to see us.

The fireflies danced

as we dined in the darkness.

After dinner
we told scary stories
and sang silly songs by the fire.

It got late.

Harry said we could sleep in his old cars.

So we did.

That night I dreamed that
the fireflies carried Harry away.

But he was back

in time to make breakfast.